Jeremy Strong

Sir Rupert and Rosie Gusset in Deadly Danger

PUFFIN BOOKS

PUFFIN BOOKS

Published by the Penguin Group
Penguin Books Ltd, 80 Strand, London WC2R 0RL, England
Penguin Putnam Inc., 375 Hudson Street, New York, New York 10014, USA
Penguin Books Australia Ltd, 250 Camberwell Road, Camberwell, Victoria 3124, Australia
Penguin Books Canada Ltd, 10 Alcorn Avenue, Toronto, Ontario, Canada M4V 3B2
Penguin Books India (P) Ltd, 11 Community Centre, Panchsheel Park,
New Delhi – 110 017, India
Penguin Books (NZ) Ltd, Cnr Rosedale and Airborne Roads, Albany,
Auckland, New Zealand
Penguin Books (South Africa) (Pty) Ltd, 24 Sturdee Avenue,
Rosebank 2196, South Africa

On the World Wide Web at: www.penguin.com

Penguin Books Ltd, Registered Offices: 80 Strand, London, WC2R 0RL England

First published by A & C Black Publishers Ltd, 1999
Published in Puffin Books, 2001
1

Text copyright © Jeremy Strong, 1999
All rights reserved

The moral right of the author has been asserted

Set in Baskerville
Typeset by Rowland Phototypesetting Ltd, Bury St Edmunds, Suffolk
Made and printed in England by Clays Ltd, St Ives plc

British Library Cataloguing in Publication Data
A CIP catalogue record for this book is available from the British Library

ISBN 0-141-30490-1

*This story is for all
sixteenth-century anorakanachronists,
but much more for those who enjoy
the simple pleasures of life,
like reading and laughing.*

Contents

1 A Very Secret Mission

Queen Margaret lay on a splendid couch, surrounded by her three most powerful ministers from the Inner Cabinet. She gazed across the room at the portrait of a good-looking young man and heaved a sigh.

'If the King of Sicily does not marry me I shall die,' she said faintly.

'I doubt it,' muttered Lord Wetwallop into his neatly pruned beard. 'Not with the amount of food you stuff into your face.'

'Did you speak, Wetwallop?'

'Indeed, Your Highness,' answered the Minister for Security, Espionage and General Villainy. 'I said that surely when this, um, king sees your portrait and realizes how beautiful you are he will be desperate to marry you.'

Queen Margaret glanced again at the

painting of the king. He was indeed a tall, dark and handsome fellow. He was brandishing a sword and pointing at a distant stag, as if he were about to leap after it, hunt it down and turn it into venison casserole on the spot. The queen sighed and then turned her gaze upon the recently completed portrait of herself, still glistening with wet paint.

This picture was a masterpiece. Not only had the artist made Queen Margaret look fifty times more beautiful than she was, she also looked twenty years younger and ten centimetres thinner. Her wiry black hair had somehow become golden ringlets. Her darting grey eyes, usually as sharp as daggers, were now blue and swooning with love. Her tight, pursed lips looked like luscious strawberries, and the fat, red pimple on her nose had become a fetching beauty spot upon her cheek.

Queen Margaret was delighted with the result, and so was the artist. When he had first started work on the portrait he had painted the queen just as she was and had almost ended up having his head chopped off. He had only saved his life by hurriedly painting the queen as the ravishing beauty she wasn't.

Sir Percy Snivel frowned and pointed out that he felt the hair colour wasn't quite right and, well . . . 'Well, what?' snapped the queen, suddenly sitting bolt upright.

'The eyes are the wrong colour too,' he said. Sir Percy liked things to be right. 'Of course the artist has used different colours,' growled the queen. 'He has painted the inner me. He has painted my beautiful soul. He has painted me as I really am, not as I appear to be on the surface.' She turned her cold eyes on the unfortunate Sir Percy. 'Of course, if he were to paint your inner soul, Sir Percy, he would probably have to paint a picture of a pig. Ha!'

'Ha, ha, ha,' echoed the rest of the Inner Cabinet, except Sir Percy.

'A pig with ears like rhubarb leaves! Ha, ha!' The other ministers smiled and laughed dutifully, while Queen Margaret rolled off her couch in hysterics. 'And a snout like, like – chocolate pudding! Hah!'

The Inner Cabinet fell silent. The chancellor, Lord Belchpot cleared his throat. 'Excuse me, Your Highness? A snout like what?'

'Chocolate pudding!' giggled the queen, climbing back on to her couch.

'I don't think anyone can have a snout like chocolate pudding,' said Lord Belchpot.

The queen fixed him with a deadly

stare. 'If I say he has a snout like chocolate pudding then that is what I mean – or perhaps you would like to see what it is like to go about with no head on your shoulders.'

'That's not possible, ma'am,' said the chancellor. 'If I had no head I wouldn't be able to go anywhere, and I wouldn't be able to see either, and anyhow I would be dead and . . .'

'SHUT UP, YOU DRIVELLING IMBECILE!'

By this time Queen Margaret was standing on her couch and stamping her feet so hard that a moment later there was a dreadful tearing sound and she disappeared up to her knees.

'Now look what you've done!' she yelled.

The Inner Cabinet shrank back from her wrath and kept very quiet. Sir Percy tried to turn the queen's thoughts on to another subject.

'I believe, ma'am, that you have sent for Sir Rupert Gusset. He is awaiting your pleasure in the Outer Chamber at this very moment.'

'Indeed,' muttered the queen, yanking one leg from the bowels of the couch, losing her balance and tumbling backwards in an unqueenly display of flying skirts and frothy knickers. 'At least there is one person in my realm that I can rely on.' The queen struggled to her feet and smoothed her dress.

'Send him in.'

Sir Rupert Gusset was a short, tubby man with an untamed beard and an untamed stomach. Even as he entered the room he felt as if a Force Ten storm was brewing throughout his insides. A rush of trapped air forced its way through his intestines, desperate for escape. Unable to

stop it, Sir Rupert gave a loud
burp, quickly followed by
something noisier, smellier,
and rather more
personal.

'If anyone else made
noises like that in my
presence I would have his
head chopped off,'
commented the queen, waving a hand in
front of her nose. 'However, as you are my
bravest and most resourceful sea captain,
you are pardoned.'

'Most kind.' Sir
Rupert's voice was a
trembling squeak.

'I have not forgotten
how you and that clever
daughter of yours, Rosie,
outwitted that dreadful
pirate, Mad Mavis, and

fought that useless Sir Sidney Dribble. Now I have a new task for you, a mission of the utmost importance and secrecy.'

Sir Rupert's entire stomach crashed into his boots, shot up to the top of his neck, almost tripped over his teeth and plunged back into his chest. His legs felt like jelly that hadn't even set. Why did he have to get mixed up in things like this? All he wanted was a quiet life back on his farm, picking lettuces and playing tiddlywinks with young Rosie, even if she did have a depressing taste for adventure on the high seas. Sir Rupert hated high seas. He wasn't very fond of low seas either, and he hated secret missions. They always meant trouble.

'Your Majesty,' murmured the brave sea captain, bowing low. 'What is your command?'

'Do you see that portrait of me over there?'

Sir Rupert gazed across the room. He could see a painting of a man waving a sword. That certainly wasn't the queen. And he could see a painting of a very attractive young lady, who most certainly didn't look like the queen either. He wondered if some dreadful trick was being played upon him and trembling, he pointed at the new portrait.

'Surely it is not you, Your Majesty?' said Sir Rupert, because it surely wasn't.

'It is me!' cried the queen with delight, thinking Sir Rupert had recognized her beautiful soul. 'Now this is your mission. I charge you to carry my portrait to the King of Sicily.' She waved at the other portrait. 'That's him over there. I am in love with him, and I want you to arrange our marriage. Show him my portrait and tell him how kind I am, how loving, how gentle and so on. You will take this coffer with you.' Queen Margaret threw back the lid of a huge oak chest. 'Inside are twenty thousand gold coins . . .'

'Your Majesty!' cried Lord Belchpot, hurrying forward. 'That's a king's ransom!'

'No, it's a queen's marriage settlement,' the queen calmly replied. 'Sir

Rupert, you will show my portrait to the King of Sicily, pay him this dowry and arrange for me to marry him. Then you will bring him back here so that we may be wed.'

Sir Rupert stared anxiously at the gold coins. 'But Your Majesty, if anyone knows I am carrying all that treasure they will surely come after me. Making me sail with such booty is like putting a noose around my neck.'

'Surely you are not afraid?' demanded the queen. 'And do please stop breaking wind. Your stomach is more stormy than the Six Seas.'

'Seven, Your Majesty.'

'Seven? There were only six last week. I do wish people would stop discovering things. Anyhow, the only people who know about this gold are the people in this room. Lord Wetwallop, my

Minister for Security, Espionage and General Villainy has kept the whole thing utterly secret.' The queen plunged a hand into the nest of hair upon her head. There was something in there jumping about and biting her, something small and flea-like . . . maybe even two or three somethings.

Sir Rupert sighed. He had another question, a rather important one. 'W–w–w–what happens if the King of Sicily doesn't want to marry you?'

'Doesn't want to marry me?' screamed the queen. 'Don't be ridiculous! Of course he will, and if he doesn't I shall die of despair, but I shall make sure that you die first, on the executioner's block. Is that clear?'

It was only too clear. With a heart full of misgivings and a stomach full of gas Sir Rupert picked up the queen's portrait and trudged dismally from the room.

'Make sure you don't smudge it!' Queen Margaret yelled after him. 'It's still wet!'

2 And Another Secret Mission . . .

Lord Wetwallop's sunken eyes flickered with hatred as he sat in his oak-panelled office. What did the queen think she was up to? What on earth did she see in that jumped-up twit of a king? As far as Lord Wetwallop was concerned, the King of Sicily was a nasty little weasel with a nose like a parsnip.

He could not understand how Queen Margaret could possibly love such a man. On the other hand, when it came to himself, well, who could ask for a finer figure?

Actually, the answer to this question was

'everyone'. Lord Wetwallop was short, grey and had a face like a sponge – a wet, mouldy, but very cunning sponge. As for his nose, it was remarkably similar to a Brussels sprout, so he was in no position to throw vegetable insults.

Lord Wetwallop was quite simply jealous. He had always rather fancied Queen Margaret himself, and there was no way he was going to let his beloved queen marry the King of Sicily. Nor was he going to let the king get his hands on those twenty thousand gold coins, because if there was one thing that Lord Wetwallop loved even more than the queen it was money, especially when it came in the tempting shape of gold coins.

No, if anyone was going to get all that treasure it would be Wetwallop himself. All he had to do was work out how to get rid of Sir Rupert Gusset, grab the loot and make sure King Parsnip-nose didn't even get a sniff of marriage. And since he was the Minister for Security, Espionage and General Villainy he knew just how to go about such villainous tasks. Lord Wetwallop smiled the sort of smile a bird-eating spider smiles when it sees a plump sparrow. He reached into a drawer, pulled out a small

silver bell and rang it gently.

Moments later, a rather ordinary-looking man walked into his office. The minister looked up and gave him his bird-eating spider smile. 'Ah, Murk, do take a seat.'

Murk Malpractice sat down without a sound. His features were as unnoticeable as a roof tile, and this exceptional plainness had been the secret of his success and had helped make him England's greatest secret agent. He had an uncanny ability to blend in with his surroundings, no matter where he was. He didn't stand out in a crowd. He didn't even stand out in an empty room, especially if he was sitting down. His complete lack of characteristics made him almost invisible.

'I have a job for you,' growled Lord Wetwallop. 'I want you to follow Sir Rupert Gusset. The queen is sending him to Sicily.

She wants to marry the king, and I don't think that would be at all . . . wise.' The minister could barely disguise his jealousy as the words hissed through his gritted teeth. 'Sir Rupert has twenty thousand gold coins on board his ship as a marriage settlement, and a portrait of the queen.

'He must be stopped! You must make sure that neither the portrait, nor the money ever reaches Sicily. Destroy the portrait and bring the money back here. We shall split it fifty-fifty, ten thousand for you and ten thousand for me.'

Murk Malpractice gave a pleased nod and got to his feet. 'What about Sir Rupert? What shall I do with him?'

'Kill him. The queen will only chop off his head when he gets back here, so you can save her the trouble. This is to be kept a total secret, is that understood?'

'Of course,' murmured Malpractice,

bowing slightly. 'Consider the job done.'

'Good. Sir Rupert will be setting sail shortly. You'd better get on his trail at once.'

Malpractice slipped silently away from the office. As soon as he had left the building he hurried to a busy tavern near by, and into a dark corner-seat where the only other occupant was a short, well-muscled sailor enveloped in a huge and ancient brown coat, even though it was mid-summer.

'Your worship?' growled Snottless, raising one hairy eyebrow. (He only had one eyebrow to raise. The other eyebrow, and the eye too, was covered by a large, blue eye-patch with yellow polka-dots. Snottless considered himself a great fashion-leader when it came to colour-coordinated eye-patches.)

'There's a job,' murmured Malpractice. 'Big money.'

'I'm listening.'

Malpractice quickly explained what he had just learned from Lord Wetwallop, except for the bit about bringing the money back. Already Murk was planning a severely sneaky trick. He wasn't going to bring back any money for Lord Wetwallop. Oh no, he was going to keep the twenty thousand for himself.

'Sir Rupert Gusset is sailing with a chest full of gold coins . . .'

'How much?' snorted Snottless, wiping a copious sleeve across his magnificently dripping nose.

'Ten thousand . . .'

'Ten thousand . . .!' Snottless's one eye lit up with delight.

'Indeed. We shall kill Sir Rupert, steal the chest and split the money fifty-fifty. That's five thousand for you, and five thousand for me.'

Snottless sniggered and threw open his coat. The insides were lined with pockets, and the pockets were jammed full of weapons – knives, swords, daggers, pistols, clubs, catapults, even a couple of huge kitchen spoons and something that looked remarkably like a potato-peeler. 'I'm going to enjoy this,' sniffed the grimy sailor, and together they slunk away, ready to track down Sir Rupert.

Sir Rupert had gone straight home from the queen's court and taken to his bed without telling anyone what had happened. Three days later he was still lying beneath the sheets and desperately hoping that it had all been a very bad dream. However, on the morning of the third day a messenger on horseback came hurtling along the muddy path that led to the brave sea captain's rambling farm.

'Post-ho! Post-ho!' yodelled the messenger as he bounced up and down in the saddle. 'Letter for Sir Rupert Gusset!'

Young Rosie Gusset came charging out of the house. It was always exciting when the post came. She took the letter and rushed indoors, while the messenger rushed on too, through a small haystack, across the chicken yard and finally straight into the duck pond, where his horse suddenly stopped dead because it was thirsty, sending him straight over the beast's head and into the water. Rosie ignored the loud splash and faint cry from outside and hurried upstairs to her father's room. 'It's a letter for you, Father, all the way from London.' Sir Rupert's pale face appeared from beneath the sheets.

'I've got the plague,' he said faintly.

'Don't be silly. Of course you haven't got the plague.'

'How do you know?'

'Because if you did have the plague you'd have boils under your armpits . . .'

'I can feel them coming up right at this moment,' muttered Sir Rupert, his hands clamped in his armpits.

'. . . and your tongue would be turning black.'

Sir Rupert grabbed a mirror and stuck out his tongue. It was a very healthy shade of pink. 'It is black,' he groaned. Rosie ignored him. She was used to this kind of behaviour. Her father always thought he was ill, especially if he knew he had to do something he didn't want to do, like washing-up, or cleaning out the chicken shed, or sailing to Sicily with twenty thousand gold coins and a portrait of the queen that didn't look a bit like her.

Rosie thrust the letter into her father's trembling hands. 'Do read it, Father. What news is there? Is it an adventure?' Sir Rupert could never understand how his young daughter could get excited by thoughts of danger when they just made him feel ill. He broke the seal, unfolded a small piece of paper and began to read. Sir Rupert turned the paper over.

Have you gone yet?
Signed: Her Royal Majesty
Queen Margaret P.T.O.

Rosie peered over her father's shoulder. 'Gone where? What's it all about,

If you haven't gone yet you
had better get a move on
at once. The Royal Executioner
has got a new axe and
he wants to try it out as soon
as possible. Love Maggie.
P.S. Don't forget to take that
clever daughter of yours, Rosie

Father? Has she sent you on a mission?
Look, she wants me to go too. Brilliant!'

With a heavy heart, Sir Rupert told
Rosie all about the secret mission. She sat
on the end of his bed and listened with
growing excitement until she could barely
contain herself. 'Where's the portrait of the
queen?' she asked.

'I put it under the bed.'

Rosie pulled out the painting,
propped it up against the old oak wardrobe

and stared with a growing smile. 'It doesn't look like her at all.'

'That's just part of the problem, Rosie. If I don't succeed I shall lose my head. What's even worse is that I shall have twenty thousand gold coins on board ship. Imagine how many people would like to get their hands on that. It's supposed to be a secret, but I don't trust any of the queen's ministers. I can smell trouble, enormous

trouble, the most gigantic trouble I have ever been in.'

Rosie squeezed one of her father's hands encouragingly. 'Don't worry, Father, Nanny and I will come with you, and then we shall all be in gigantic trouble together.'

3 A Fateful Meeting

Rosie Gusset's nanny had big shoulders, a big bosom and a big bottom. She had big strong arms and big strong legs. Nanny was the ex All-Europe Women's Wrestling Champion, and she had a gold trophy to prove it. She had given up wrestling and taken on the job of looking after Rosie, whose real mother had died when she was eight. Nanny loved Rosie as if she were her own daughter.

She was also extremely good at growing vegetables in the big garden behind the farmhouse. Rosie and Nanny used to spend hours out there, nattering away to each other, so it was hardly surprising that Nanny was the first person to hear about Sir Rupert's secret mission.

'Ooh, Rosie, your father won't like that!'

Rosie nodded sadly. 'He already thinks he's got the plague.'

'Never you mind, my lovely little cheesecake, we'll soon have him strutting about the deck of *The Lame Duck* acting the hero.' Nanny flexed her muscles and smiled. 'We haven't had an adventure since that jolly time with Mad Mavis the Pirate Queen and Sir Sidney Dribble. It's about time we went to sea again.'

'Father doesn't think so. In fact, I don't know why he ever became a sailor. He doesn't seem to like the sea at all.'

'Piddling pea-pods,' laughed Nanny. 'Your father's got the sea in his blood. He just likes making a bit of a fuss, that's all.' Nanny bent down and whispered in Rosie's ear. 'But don't you worry, he'll soon be throwing his weight around.'

There certainly seemed to be some truth in Nanny's remarks because as soon as they reached port and began preparing for the voyage ahead, Sir Rupert took control. He stood on the poop deck of *The Lame Duck*, leaning over the railings and shouting to the crew.

'Muggins, have you got the food stowed somewhere dry?'

The First Mate saluted Sir Rupert. 'Indeed I have, Cap'n, an' there's enough biscuits to keep us goin' for a hundred years.'

'I do hope the journey won't take that long,' groaned Sir Rupert, who thought a hundred hours would be more than he could bear.

Muggins rubbed his bristly chin. 'Ah, well now, sir, you can never have enough biscuits. Just supposin' we all get shipwrecked and marooned on a distant shore with nothin' but sand an' rocks? A biscuit can be like a blessing from 'eaven.'

The thought of this turned Sir Rupert

so pale he felt faint. He hurriedly sat down on a capstan and put his head between his knees. Nanny clapped an outsized hand upon his back and almost sent him flying into the deep harbour waters.

'Don't you worry your noddle, Sir Rupert, I'm sure everything will be fine. Rosie and I will look after you.'

Strenuous creaking came from above as thick ropes swung into action, lifting Queen Margaret's great treasure chest from

the dock-side and on board *The Lame Duck*.
The First Mate eyed Sir Rupert and the
swinging coffer suspiciously.

''Scuse me, Cap'n, but can you tell me
what might be in that there chest?'

'That I cannot, Muggins, except to say
that in that chest is a secret that we shall
take to our graves, if necessary.'

Muggins frowned and the crew pressed
around him, muttering. After several
moments the First Mate turned back to Sir
Rupert. ''Scuse me, Cap'n, but the crew say
would you mind if they don't go to their
graves just yet awhile? They'd rather go
'ome to their families as it 'appens, families
bein' a bit more comforting than coffins, if
you see what they mean . . .'

Sir Rupert saw exactly what they
meant. He agreed with them
wholeheartedly, but he was also a loyal
subject of Queen Margaret.

'Have no fear, Muggins, and stow the chest below. I want an armed guard to keep watch over it day and night.' Muggins's eyes widened. An armed guard could only mean one thing.

'I suppose that'll be treasure inside then, Cap'n?'

'Ssssh! Do you think I want the whole port to know?'

Muggins winked and leaned forward confidentially. 'Don't you worry, Cap'n. It'll just be you, me, an' everyone else on board who knows about the treasure.' Sir Rupert suddenly felt desperately ill, again.

Unbeknown to Sir Rupert and his crew, they were being carefully watched by two men, hiding behind a large pile of barrels on the quayside. One of the men merged into his surroundings, whilst the other – a short, badly shaven sailor wearing an ancient coat

that seemed several sizes too large – peered
between the barrels.

'They're definitely getting ready to sail,
your worship,' muttered Snottless.

'So it would seem,' Murk Malpractice
agreed, 'and somehow we must follow them.'

'Perhaps we could get ourselves taken
on as crew?' suggested Snottless.

'Hmmm. That's one possibility, but
then what would we do?'

'Ah,' growled Snottless, showing a row
of black teeth in an unpleasant smile. 'Well
now, sire, I have a rather clever idea.'

'Oh yes?'

'Yes. We get on
board Sir Rupert's
ship, wait until we
are at sea and
then scuttle her.'

'Scuttle
her?' Malpractice

appeared rather surprised by this unusual plan.

'Yes, sire. We make a hole in the bottom of her hull and down she goes, to the bottom of the sea.'

Malpractice gazed steadily at his assistant for some while. 'Yes,' he said at last. 'Sadly there are at least two problems with this idea of yours, Snottless.'

'Is that so, sire?'

'Yes. First of all, the general idea is to steal the queen's treasure. Forgive me if I am wrong here, but if *The Lame Duck* sinks to the bottom of the sea, then the treasure sinks with her.'

'Ah . . .' The smile faded from Snottless's grimy face.

'And secondly, since we too are on board *The Lame Duck*, which will now be lying on the seabed, we shall have drowned, shall we not?'

Snottless chewed his dirty fingernails.
'Not such a good idea after all then.'

'Not really. But do try again sometime
– maybe when you find yourself a brain –
preferably a human brain and not the one
you are using at present, which appears to
belong to a cuttlefish.'

Murk drummed his elegant fingers on
one of the barrels as he considered the
problems facing the pair of them. At present
they were outnumbered, and that was of
grave concern to him. Also, it was important

that when the time came to attack and steal
the treasure, nobody could trace the crime
back to himself.

'Snottless, are there any other ships in
harbour at present?'

'There are a couple of trading galleons
in from the Azores and freshly unloaded.'

'One of those might do nicely. Come
on, we have some bargaining to do.'

The two men slipped away and
headed for the nearest vessel. It was a tiny,
battered wreck of a ship named *The Jellyfish*,
held together it seemed with bent nails and
prayers. Murk strode up the gangplank and
asked for the captain. He could not disguise
his surprise and delight when a tall figure
appeared – a tall, thin, snooty figure to be
exact, with shifty eyes and a nose as long
and curved as a shark's fin.

'What a glorious twist of fate has
brought us together, brave sir,' cried

Malpractice, holding out his hand. 'If I am not mistaken you are Sir Sidney Dribble, the famous poet and adventurer.'

'Indeed I am Sir Sidney, my dear sir, but ever since my boat – *The Windbag* – was mashed to bits in an ocean battle I have fallen on hard times. This . . .', here Sir Sidney waved a dramatic arm around his little ship, '. . . is all I have to sail in these days – nothing but a dirty little trading pot.' Sir Sidney paused and eyed his visitor intently. 'I have written a poem about my trials in this cruel world. Would you like to hear it?' And before Murk could stop him, Sir Sidney threw out his arms and launched into verse.

'Wild winds work the Storms of Life that crash
    about our feeble heads –
Like crashing waves that crash about, crashing,
    crashing, crash, crash, crash.'

Sir Sidney stopped and looked to see what

effect his poem had worked upon his audience. They stared back at him, lost for words, and Sir Sidney took this to mean that they were overwhelmed. 'Of course it isn't finished yet. I am planning another eighty lines, but I do like that bit with all the crashing, don't you? I put it in as a kind of sound effect because waves do crash a bit, don't they?'

Malpractice nodded weakly. He hastily took Sir Sidney by the elbow and guided him down to the captain's cabin, leaving Snottless to guard the door. As soon as they were out of earshot of the rest of the crew, Malpractice got down to business.

'Tell me, Sir Sidney, what do you think of Sir Rupert Gusset?'

Sir Sidney leaped to his feet, drawing his sword and swishing it round his head. 'That tubby little windbreaker! I'd like to have his guts for garters! He's the one that landed me in this God-forsaken old tub – he sank *The Windbag* with potatoes!'

'You don't like him then?' asked Malpractice. Sir Sidney didn't answer. He just turned a deep shade of the most angry purple, viciously drove his sword into a plump cushion and twisted it about several times, sending a cloud of feathers swirling into the air. Murk Malpractice observed Sir Sidney's anger and smiled. This was going to be easy. 'I would like to help you get rid of Sir Rupert.'

At once Sir Sidney's eyes turned from hatred to a weasel-glint. He hastily sat down. 'Quick, tell me how to do it. I'll do anything!'

Half an hour later, *The Jellyfish* set sail in hot pursuit of *The Lame Duck*, armed to the teeth with twenty cannons.

4 Dressing-up Time

With no idea that big trouble was fast
catching up with them, the crew of *The
Lame Duck* were enjoying being at sea once
again. The wind was fresh and clean and
whipped spray from the sea in silver puffs of
glittering stars. Several dolphins had joined
the ship and for the last hour they had been
leaping and rolling just ahead of *The Lame
Duck*'s dipping prow. Rosie and Nanny
leaned over one side of the ship, watching
them. Sir Rupert leaned over the other side,
being sick.

'I'm dying,' he groaned. 'I wish I was
a lump of rock.'

'And why would you be wanting to be
a rock then?' Nanny couldn't resist asking.

'Because,' hiccuped the brave
explorer, 'rocks don't do anything. Rocks

don't have to go on dangerous missions. They don't get seasick. They're just – rocks.' Sir Rupert's stomach lurched into a renewed bout of volcanic activity. When it was over he slithered to the deck in a sad, damp heap, muttering to himself. 'I want to be a rock. Just a small one will do nicely. I'm not ambitious.'

Rosie crouched down beside her father and cradled his head. 'You'll soon find your sea-legs, Father. Come on, I'll help you to your cabin. Nanny, give me a hand.' Nanny lifted Sir Rupert in her huge arms, tossed him over one shoulder and set off for the captain's cabin. Halfway there, a rousing cry came from the lookout.

The crew hurried to the port rail and gazed across the water. Sure enough, in the distance there was a boat turning towards them and piling on sail, with the obvious intention of catching *The Lame Duck*.

'Who could that be?' asked Rosie.
Nanny shook her big head.

'I don't know, my dumpling. What do
you think, Sir Rupert?'

Poor Sir Rupert had no idea at all.
Draped as he was over Nanny's back, the
only thing he could see was her immense
bottom. 'Put me down,' he pleaded. Once
he was safely on his feet he watched the

distant vessel slowly close on
them. He was filled with
foreboding.

'Pirates,' muttered
Muggins. 'Could be
pirates, Cap'n, come to
steal our gold.'

'That's a secret, Muggins,' hissed Sir
Rupert.

'Whoever it is, they do look as if
they're spoiling for a fight,' Rosie said, and
the crew began whispering darkly to the
First Mate.

'I can't believe a tiny
tub like that would
want to fight us,'
murmured Sir
Rupert.

''Scuse me, Cap'n,'
Muggins interrupted,
'but the crew say if

there's going to be a fight can we make sail and run away?'

Rosie was outraged. 'Muggins! You're supposed to be brave sailors!'

'Ah yes, miss, an' that we are too. 'Earts like lions, we 'ave. It's just our legs that aren't so brave, you see, an' they do so like to go running in the opposite direction.'

Muggins's brave speech was rudely interrupted by the loud boom of a cannon, and moments later a fountain of water spouted from the sea just ahead of *The Lame Duck*. In an instant the dolphins dived and vanished. If those strange humans were going to start throwing big lumpy things at each other, they didn't want to know.

On board *The Jellyfish*, Murk Malpractice was overseeing the firing of the ship's cannons. Before leaving harbour the secret agent had cunningly purchased an extra twenty cannons. 'Sir Rupert will never expect a small, battered trading vessel like *The Jellyfish* to be armed to the teeth,' he told Snottless. 'The old fool will be taken completely by surprise. He doesn't stand a chance!' As the cannons went into action, he turned his attention to Sir Sidney. 'Now, Sir Sidney, I think it would be wise if you adopted a disguise.'

'Really?'

'We don't want Sir Rupert to know who we are,' Malpractice pointed out.

'But I do,' Sir Sidney protested. 'I want my moment of triumph! I want Sir Rupert to see that it is me that has reduced him to a snivelling bit of flotsam.'

'Your time for that will come,' Malpractice promised, 'but in order to maintain our surprise you must disguise yourself. I don't think Sir Rupert will recognize me, but he knows you only too well.'

Sir Sidney considered the idea carefully. 'I could be a rabbit,' he suggested. 'I do very good rabbit impressions. Children always like them at parties.' He stuck two hands up from the back of his head and waved them a few times, while attempting to wiggle his nose.

'I don't think the rabbit is frightening enough,' hinted Malpractice and hurriedly took a step back as Sir Sidney threw himself to the floor, humped his back and began lurching across the deck.

'How about a caterpillar? Not an ordinary one though, I'll be scary – this one is poisonous,' said Sir Sidney, and he hissed. 'Sssss.' Snottless was impressed and leaped back as Sir Sidney tried to nibble his sea-boots. Murk shook his head.

'I have a better idea. Why not dress up as a pirate?'

'Oh yes!' cried Snottless, as Sir Sidney struggled to his feet. 'That's very clever. A pirate would be just right.'

'And I know just which pirate you should be,' smiled the secret agent. 'Mad Mavis.' Sir Sidney's jaw dropped and his thin nose began to tremble indignantly.

'Mad Mavis the pirate? Mad Mavis the WOMAN!???!'

'Exactly.'

'I can't be a woman!' cried Sir Sidney.

'Don't you see what a brilliant disguise it would be? Sir Rupert will recognize Mad Mavis at once. Everyone knows how wicked she is, and Mad Mavis will get the blame for stealing the treasure chest. Think of all that gold,' whispered Murk, who knew a thing or two about human nature.

Sir Sidney stared moodily at the distant shape of *The Lame Duck*. 'All right.

I'll do it,' grunted the poet, and he went below to find some suitable clothes.

It must be said that Mad Mavis, who was just about the most infamous pirate there was, did not look one bit like Sir Sidney. Mad Mavis was large and fat. Sir Sidney was tall and thin; he also had a beard. Mad Mavis didn't have a beard, although she did have a moustache.

Nevertheless, Sir Sidney did his best, and after a short while he appeared back on the deck of *The Jellyfish* wearing a huge black cape. He had stuffed pillows up his front and down inside his pantaloons to fatten himself up. He had wound a big black scarf round most of his face to hide his shark's nose and wispy beard. And he sported a huge black hat with a wide, floppy brim.

Snottless took one look and ran away yelling, whilst Murk just about managed to stop himself giggling. Sir Sidney was very pleased with the overall effect.

'What do you think?'

'Mad Mavis is much shorter. Get down on your knees.'

Sir Sidney fell to his knees and shuffled across the deck while the agent watched carefully. With Mad Mavis in place and *The Lame Duck* already being bombarded all was going to plan. 'Yes, that's much better. Right then, time to close in and finish off the enemy. On my order, round three, cannons fire!'

Clouds of thick grey smoke belched from the mouths of the cannons and were carried away on the wind. As soon as one cannon had been fired it was rolled back, quickly reloaded, pushed out through the open gun-port and fired again. Flames burst from the barrels as cannonballs hurtled towards Sir Rupert's treasure-ship.

It would only be a matter of time before she was hit, holed, disabled, destroyed, smashed about a bit and seriously sunk.

5 Let Battle Commence!

Sir Rupert watched white-faced as the enemy closed in. That beaten-up trading galleon must have at least thirty cannons on board. What on earth was it up to? Pillars of water were shooting up all around *The Lame Duck*. One cannonball went screeching through a sail, leaving a gaping hole. Suddenly Rosie spied something black jerking up the enemy's main mast and fluttering menacingly in the stiff wind. 'The Jolly Roger!' she cried. 'Pirates!'

'I said it was pirates,' grumbled Muggins.

'All this banging and shouting is giving me the most awful headache,' said Sir Rupert, 'I can't think straight.' But Rosie had no time for headaches.

'Load the cannons and return fire!' she ordered.

'Aye-aye, miss.' Muggins hurried away, and as their own cannons began to boom back at the enemy Nanny clutched at Rosie's shoulder.

'Look, my pudding, there on the quarter-deck. I do believe that's Mad Mavis.'

Rosie stared at the black, caped figure. 'So it is!'

On board *The Jellyfish*, Sir Sidney shuffled along on his knees and hailed Sir Rupert. 'Ahoy there! Heave to and let us board. I am Mad Mavis, the most feared pirate on the Six Seas . . .'

'Seven,' Sir Rupert shouted back.

'What?'

'There are seven.'

'I don't believe you; name them,' demanded Sir Sidney crossly.

Malpractice growled at his ally. 'We

are in the middle of a sea battle, Sir Sidney. We are trying to get our hands on twenty thousand gold coins, just in case you had forgotten. Tell them to surrender.'

'All right, but I still don't believe him.' Sir Sidney turned seaward and bellowed across the water. 'Take in your sail or you'll be sunk without fail.' Sir Sidney beamed and rose to his feet. 'I say, that rhymes! In the heat of battle I am composing poetry. What a genius I am. Did you . . .'

The secret agent threw himself upon the poet, dragging him down on to the deck. 'You'll give yourself away,' he hissed. 'Get down on your knees.'

But on board *The Lame Duck*, Rosie was already wondering. 'Did you see that? Mad Mavis just doubled in size, and then some man jumped on her.'

'Don't be silly, squirrel. Nobody jumps on Mad Mavis, not man, woman nor flea.

It's more than life is worth, jumping on Mad Mavis.'

But Rosie was not to be put off. 'Nanny,' she declared, 'somebody jumped on her, and pulled her down again.'

'All right, all right,' murmured Nanny soothingly. 'But let me ask you something – how come that battered old trading barge has so much cannon on board?'

Rosie gave the pirate boat another searching look and quickly spotted the obvious. 'It's not Mad Mavis's ship. Her ship's called the *Bucket o' Blood* and that one's name is *The Jellyfish*. How peculiar. Come on, battle-stations! They're closing fast. Muggins – stand by for hand-to-hand fighting!'

The sea was foaming with shot from both vessels, but most of it was coming from *The Jellyfish* and she certainly had the treasure boat at a severe disadvantage, outnumbering her cannons by three to one. Several sails on board *The Lame Duck* were now peppered with holes, so she couldn't even make much speed. It was becoming clear that *The Lame Duck* would soon come to a halt altogether and then the pirates would be able to swarm on board. She was at their mercy.

It was at this desperate point in the battle that fate smiled down upon *The Lame Duck* and its hapless crew. Unfortunately for Sir Sidney his ancient tub was falling to bits. It had dry rot and wet rot. It even had slightly damp rot. Deck-boards had a nasty habit of suddenly giving way as you walked across them, plunging you into the hold of the ship, and that is exactly what happened next.

Three crew members had reloaded one of the biggest cannons and just as they lit the firing fuse the floorboards beneath the cannon gave way with a great crack. All at once the cannon tipped backwards and disappeared into a gaping hole. As it vanished the barrel boomed and fired its missile. The cannonball whizzed straight up through the deck and completely demolished the main mast.

The mast crashed down upon the rotten deck and plunged into the hold. Meanwhile the vast sails that were attached to the mast now flapped and flopped over half the boat so that nobody could see what they were doing or where they were going. *The Jellyfish* began to go round and round in a tight circle while the dirty white blanket of sail

that now covered the boat heaved with
wriggling pirates, struggling to climb
out from beneath it.

'They're getting
away!' moaned Sir
Sidney in despair. 'Oh,
this is so tragic! My greatest enemy is sailing
away and he's still got the gold. Bitter, bitter
world!'

'You're not going to recite a poem, are
you?' muttered Snottless, slipping a hand
inside his coat and fingering a pistol, just in
case.

Malpractice peered out from beneath
the canvas and watched *The Lame Duck*
slowly escape. 'Don't worry, my tragic friend.
We shall repair the boat and sail on. Sir
Rupert may have got away this time, but
only through sheer good luck. Next time we
shall make sure that all the luck is on our
side. He's as good as done for!'

Sicily glittered and shone in the sunshine as *The Lame Duck*, now with big brown patches on its sails, slowly made its way into the busy little harbour. The King of Sicily was evidently a powerful ruler, because most of the boats moored in the harbour appeared to be warships. 'I wouldn't like to have one of those coming after me,' Rosie whispered in awe. 'They've got two decks of cannons.'

Nanny lifted her gaze to the town, looking at the higgledy-piggledy buildings as they rose up the steep hillside. Her eyes came to rest upon the great castle that

dominated the whole bay. 'I bet that's got more than three bedrooms,' she said.

'It is a bit grim,' Rosie answered.

The castle walls rose straight and sheer until they were crowned by massive battlements. Small, distant figures of guards could be seen patrolling the parapets.

Sir Rupert's health had improved remarkably ever since they had sighted land, and even more now that *The Lame Duck* was actually tied to the stone jetty. The hot Sicilian sun warmed his balding head as he strode about the poop deck.

'Muggins, I want you to go ashore and seek an audience for me with the king. Inform His Majesty that I am here as an envoy of Queen Margaret, and that I have a personal message for him and bear gifts from Her Majesty.'

'That I will, Cap'n.'

The First Mate set off for the castle

while the rest of the crew set about making
proper repairs to the rather battered *Lame
Duck*. Sir Rupert retired to his cabin to keep
an eye on the great oaken chest.

'We have almost completed our
mission, Rosie,' he beamed.

'But, Father, suppose those pirates
come after us again?'

'No matter. We will have handed over
the gold to the King of Sicily. You see, Rosie,
I have a sneaking suspicion that Mad Mavis
knew all about the gold we have on board,

and that is why she attacked. Once we no longer have it, she won't be interested.'

'That Mad Mavis,' hissed Nanny. 'I'd like to sit on top of her and bounce every breath out of her fat body, that I would, Sir Rupert.'

But Rosie was puzzled. 'How did Mad Mavis find out about the gold, Father? You said it was a secret, so who told her? And why wasn't she sailing in *The Bucket o' Blood*? I don't think it was Mad Mavis at all.'

Sir Rupert's mouth fell open and even Nanny's eyes popped a bit. 'Now come, come, my little fruit salad, don't you start going on about that again.'

'Going on about what?' croaked Sir Rupert, feeling that familiar sinking sensation in his stomach, and wishing he hadn't asked.

Rosie shrugged. 'I don't really know. It's just that there was something odd about the way she acted. She was walking in a very strange way . . .'

'That was the movement of the boat,' suggested Sir Rupert hopefully, but his daughter shook her head.

'No. It was too much of a waddle, and Mad Mavis definitely doesn't waddle.'

'Well if it wasn't Mad Mavis, who was it?' demanded Nanny crossly.

Rosie chewed her lip and she thought as hard as she could. Then all at once she realized. 'It was someone who wants us to think that it was Mad Mavis.'

Nanny gasped, and Sir Rupert buried his face in his hands.

'I've got the measly mump-pox,' he groaned. 'My temperature's going up . . . it's a fever for sure . . . spots in front of my eyes, squiggly dots dancing about . . . I'm dying.' He clasped his chest. 'I think my ribs are going soft and squidgy.'

This death scene was rudely shattered by Muggins, bursting through the cabin door. ''Scuse me, Cap'n, but the King of Sicily says he likes presents an' you're to bring them at once before he gets cross an' throws you to the lions.'

'Lions?' repeated Nanny. 'He's got lions?'

'He's got a whole zoo up there,' said the First Mate, 'with roarin' tigers too, an' a giant helephant, an' a chargin' rhinopuss, an' gnashin' crocodillos.' Muggins wiped the sweat from his brow and frowned as he tried

to remember something.
'An' a budgie,' he
added at length.

Sir Rupert
dragged himself to his feet. 'Get
the crew to carry this chest,' he
sighed. 'Muggins, you take Queen
Margaret's portrait. Come on,
everybody, it's time to go and do business
with the King of Sicily, and let's hope his
lions aren't hungry.'

6 Introducing His Royal Highness – the King

Muggins was quite correct about all the animals. The crew staggered up the steep and narrow streets of the town with the treasure chest and passed through the stupendous castle gates. Then they made their way amongst the animal cages that made up the king's private menagerie.

Rosie stopped to admire several pink flamingos feeding at the edge of a small lake. 'Aren't they pretty?' she began, but the words died in her throat as a huge pair of razor-toothed jaws suddenly rose from beneath the water, snatched an entire flamingo and vanished beneath the surface, dragging the poor bird with it.

'Crocodillo,' Muggins observed. 'It's their lunchtime.'

'Oh dear,' groaned Sir Rupert. Rosie slipped one hand into his.

'Come on, Father, you've almost completed the queen's mission, you said so yourself.'

Sir Rupert managed a weak smile despite his churning stomach. As they were ushered into the castle's Great Hall he tried to strike a brave pose and pressed his knees together so that they were unable to tremble quite so obviously.

The crew placed the treasure chest to one side, and Sir Rupert held the queen's portrait with a cloth cover thrown over it. Four trumpeters stepped forward and delivered an ear-splitting fanfare. At the far end of the hall a pair of huge silk curtains parted and several elegant courtiers emerged, holding up a canopy with rich

drapes. All that could be seen beneath the canopy were a pair of bejewelled feet that evidently belonged to the king. The trumpeters blasted everyone's ears again, the drapes parted and the King of Sicily emerged.

Sir Rupert had to stop himself from staring, because the King of Sicily was not at all like his portrait. He was not tall, dark and handsome. Tall? Yes. Dark? Yes, if a deep suntan can be called dark. Handsome? Not exactly. In fact he was unbelievably ugly. He had a massive donkey-jaw and browny-black teeth that projected from a cavernous, roaring mouth.

His eyes were so far apart they were almost on the sides of his face. His hair looked like mattress stuffing, and not only did it cling to his flaking scalp, it also protruded in tufts from his nostrils and ears.

The king was not only ugly, he was also huge. He had muscles the size of melons. He was the sort of person whose sheer size made you tremble; the kind of person you tried to make sure was your friend and not your enemy.

Sir Rupert was horrified. Rosie and Nanny weren't very happy either. They knew that they had just come face to face with a big problem. Queen Margaret would never want to marry such a hideous hulk, but they could hardly tell that to the king. And what about the gold? It was right there, sitting beside them in the chest.

The King of Sicily threw his arms wide and beamed at his guests. 'Welcome to Seee-seelee,' he cried. 'An' how eez your queenie? Whatta she want? Where zee prezzies? I like-a prezzies . . .'

This was the moment of truth. There was no escape. Sir Rupert shuffled forward miserably. 'Queen Margaret sends you her dearest regards, Your Majesty.'

'Show me zee prezzies!' roared the king, and Sir Rupert hastily began to uncover the portrait.

'This is a picture of Her Majesty, Your

Majesty. She wishes to marry you!'

The King of Sicily took one look and almost spat on the floor. 'Pah! She too thin. She 'ave face like-a pizza . . ., 'am an' tomato pizza.'

Sir Rupert squirmed. This was not going at all well. 'Please, Your M-M-Majesty . . .' he stammered. 'Take a closer look, I beg you.'

The king strode towards the painting and then suddenly caught sight of Nanny. He stopped dead in his tracks. His eyes bulged and he clutched his heart with both hands. 'Bee-ootiful lidee!' he cried, lurching forward and seizing Nanny in his arms. 'I kissa your leeps – ssshhhhlllurrrp! I kissa your neck – shhhhllloooppy-ssshhlllluppp! I kissa your . . .'

'Gerroff!' cried Nanny, blushing from head to toe and pushing the king away. 'You can't marry me – I'm just the nanny.'

She turned angrily on Rosie. 'And you can stop your giggling, young lady,' she muttered.

'But I love-a you,' declared the king. 'My heart explode if you do notta marry me.'

'Well I'm sure that will be very interesting to watch,' declared Nanny, patting her hair back into place. The king sighed and turned back to the brave sea captain.

'An' what else eez zair for me? Eez ziss all?'

'Indeed not, Your Majesty. Queen Margaret would like you to take this chest full of gold coins as a marriage settlement.' Sir Rupert was now hoping that the treasure would entice the king into marrying Queen Margaret.

Muggins threw open the lid of the coffer and twenty thousand coins sparkled

in the flickering light. The king lurched
forward, crashing to his knees in front of
the chest and plunging his hands into the
gold.

'Oh bee-ootiful money! I kissa ziss
coin – sshhllurrrpp! I kissa ziss coin . . .'

Sir Rupert sighed. This really was too
much. 'Do I take it that you agree to the

queen's proposal of marriage, Your
Majesty?' The king rose to his feet and
smiled rather horribly at Sir Rupert.

'No,' he snapped. 'I do not weesha to
marry your queenie. You tell her she ugly
woman.'

Sir Rupert almost choked. How on
earth was he going to tell her that? 'Please,
please marry her,' he pleaded with
desperation.

'I no like-a pizza-face,' the king went
on. 'But I do like-a prezzie. I keep ze
money.'

'But you can't! I mean, that's not fair.
You only get the money if you marry the
queen, that's the deal,' raved Sir Rupert.
Things were going from bad to worse. He
fingered his neck, as if he could already feel
the executioner's axe.

'Shuttuppa your big baby babble. I
keep ze money. 'Owever, I nice-a person, I

kind person, so you go before I feed you to lions an' tigers. Go, Go! G O!'

Sir Rupert turned and beat a hasty retreat from the Great Hall. His position was quite hopeless. With bowed head he made his weary way back to *The Lame Duck* while Rosie and Nanny whispered urgently to each other, trying to think of a way out of their dreadful situation.

Meanwhile, in a rather more seedy area of the town, *The Jellyfish* limped into a small and very smelly harbour for fishing boats. Murk Malpractice set the grumbling crew to repairing the ship while he, Snottless and Sir Sidney entered the town to spy out the land.

They arrived just in time to see Sir Rupert return to his boat in the main harbour. Malpractice noted the look of utter despair upon Sir Rupert's face.

'Something's gone wrong,' he muttered. 'They've delivered the portrait and the gold, but the king has said "no", or worse still, maybe he's not the wonderful match that Queen Margaret thinks he is, and he's decided to keep the gold. No wonder Sir Rupert looks so miserable.'

'That's just guesswork,' sniffed Sir Sidney, who was so wrapped up in himself that he never noticed what anyone else was feeling.

Snottless dragged a dirty brown sleeve across his bubbling nose. 'You just see if his worship isn't right. He's always right,' he added with resentful pride.

Sir Sidney sighed. 'Well, what's the plan?'

Murk gazed up towards the castle. 'I'm certain the gold is up there. We shall have to steal it.'

'Are you mad?'

'It shouldn't be too difficult.'

'Of course not. We just walk in and take it.'

'Not quite; you walk in . . .'

'Me!' squeaked Sir Sidney.

'Yes, you. You are going to entertain the king while we steal the gold.'

'And how am I going to do that?'

Malpractice smiled. 'I have heard that the king of Sicily is very fond of the ladies. You will disguise yourself . . .'

'No, please,' protested the poet, but

Malpractice continued relentlessly.

'. . . disguise yourself as a beautiful woman . . .'

'A WOMAN – AGAIN!!! Oh this is too much!'

Snottless began to snigger. 'Come on, Sir Sidney, it's time to go shopping for a nice dress.'

As Sir Sidney began to wail a protest the two agents took an arm each and dragged him away for a bit of off-the-peg shopping. Some local shopkeepers were surprised to find three men rummaging amongst the ladies' clothing, but they didn't mind taking money from anyone, so they kept quiet.

As evening began to fall, Murk and Snottless set about their final task – changing Sir Sidney into a beautiful damsel. It was not without a struggle that the poet gave up his beard, but when he finally emerged he was a changed man. Despite his shark's fin nose he actually looked quite lady-like. He now wore a fetching green gown, with some glittering jewellery. His long, lank hair was newly washed, piled upon his head and covered with a delicate lace shawl. Malpractice surveyed his handiwork with deep satisfaction. Sir Sidney had been transformed.

'We stay on board until dark,' Malpractice said. 'Then, around midnight, we go into action. Sir Sidney, you will go in search of the king.'

'But what shall I do when I have found him?'

'Just keep him entertained long

enough for Snottless and myself to steal the treasure chest, then hot foot it back to the boat. We'll leave some crew on board with orders to sail as soon as we are all back. We'll have the treasure and be away from the island before anyone realizes a thing!'

7 Some Good Ideas All Round

While an air of triumph filled the cabin of *The Jellyfish*, the atmosphere on board *The Lame Duck* was overflowing with despair. Sir Rupert Gusset lay in his wooden bed with the sheets pulled up over his face as if he were already dead.

'The king doesn't want to marry her and he's keeping the gold. What will I tell Her Majesty? She'll have me executed for certain.'

'Don't you worry, Sir Rupert, I'm sure we'll think of something,' said Nanny cheerfully, although her own head was as empty of ideas as a washbasin.

'I think I'm getting distemper,' groaned Sir Rupert from beneath his funeral pall.

'Don't be silly, Father. Only dogs can

get distemper. Anyhow, all is not lost. The gold is in the chest and the chest is in the castle. All we have to do is get it back.'

'Now that is a good idea,' said Nanny, brightening up at once. 'But how will we do that, my darling doughnut?'

Rosie thought hard. 'If we are going to steal back the gold we're going to need some kind of distraction,' said Rosie, looking steadily at Nanny.

'What?' said the ex All-Europe Women's Wrestling Champion. 'What are you looking at me like that for?' Rosie smiled and Nanny frowned. Rosie smiled even more and then Nanny's jaw dropped and she began waving her hands in front of her. 'Oh no, no, Rosie, I couldn't. It would be like getting into a cage with a gorilla.'

Rosie laughed. 'Please, Nanny, it would only be for a short while, just long enough to distract the king so that we can steal the treasure back. Please.'

Nanny pressed her lips together hard as she thought, and at last she nodded. 'All right, but I'm only doing it to save you and your father,' she declared.

'Oh I know,' nodded Rosie seriously. Then she smiled again. 'I kissa your leeps, I kissa your knees . . .!'

'You leave my knees out of it,' cried Nanny, turning very red indeed.

Sir Rupert slowly pulled the sheet away from his face, raised himself on one elbow and gazed at his daughter with a flicker of hope in his eyes.

'Do you really think it will work, Rosie?'

'It's our only chance, Father. I don't know if it will work or not, but we certainly can't sit here doing nothing.'

Spurred on by his daughter's determination, Sir Rupert stumbled out to the quarterdeck. He tried to strike a brave pose as he addressed the crew. 'Now then, men, we have a bit of a problem. The King of Sicily doesn't want to marry our queen and he's decided to keep the gold. You know what that means – if we go home without the gold we'll all lose our heads.'

The crew began muttering and Muggins stepped forward. ''Scuse me, Cap'n, but the crew says why don't we go somewhere else then, where we don't have to lose our heads?'

'We can't stay away from home for ever,' answered Sir Rupert. 'Rosie here has thought up a very good plan. I want some of the crew to stay here on board *The Lame Duck* and prepare to leave harbour as quickly as possible.'

'An' what about the rest of the crew, Cap'n?' Muggins asked.

'The rest will come with me, sneak into the castle at dead of night, steal the treasure chest and bring it back to the ship. Volunteers – step forward!'

Every member of the crew took one step back, and since those at the rear were already at the edge of the deck they stepped into thin air and landed in the water with several loud plops.

Rosie angrily gripped the wooden railings in front of her. 'You're all cowards!' she cried. 'My father is braver than the whole lot of you put together. Even Nanny and I are going. Are you telling me that none of you are as brave as a ten-year-old girl?'

Muggins scratched his head sheepishly, drew his sword and looked at the crew. 'Well now, miss,' he said, 'the men an' I, you see, we thought you was eleven, but since you're only ten I'm sure we'll 'ave some volunteers. Step forward, Puffkin, an' you, Throttle, an' you, Pimbeard, Farpole, Jimbo an' Crumblebottom. There you are, Cap'n, there's your volunteers.' Muggins smiled proudly and put away his sword.

'Thank you, Muggins. I'm putting you in charge of them.'

'Ah, Cap'n, I don't think it works like

that, you see, cos I don't know if you noticed, but I didn't step forward – it was jus' Puffkin, Throttle, Pimbeard an' . . .'

'We're very proud of you, Muggins,' interrupted Rosie. 'When Queen Margaret hears about this she will probably want to reward all of you.'

The men looked at each other and began grinning and pointing at their chests. 'Medals,' muttered some and they turned to their less fortunate companions who hadn't volunteered and began boasting about their exploits even though they hadn't actually done anything yet. Rosie smiled and left them to it. There was still a lot of preparation to make before darkness came down upon them.

Meanwhile, the sneaky plotters from *The Jellyfish* were creeping across town. 'Don't go so fast,' grumbled Sir Sidney. 'I keep tripping on this stupid gown.' Malpractice paused so that he could catch up.

'Make sure you keep the king occupied as long as possible,' said Murk, as he and Sir Sidney and Snottless darted from shadow to shadow, working their way towards the dark and looming castle. 'Keep your voice high and ladylike and whatever you do, don't spout poetry at him.'

'Why not?'

Malpractice grinned. 'It will only make the king more romantic.'

'If he comes anywhere near me I shall scream.'

'Good woman,' smiled Snottless.

'I'm not a woman!' squawked Sir Sidney, hitting him on the arm with his fan. 'You wait till I get my beard back.'

They sneaked through the castle gates and slipped between the animal cages. Suddenly Malpractice spotted the king wandering in his menagerie. They watched in silence as the king paused by the lions' cage and began throwing them lumps of meat. 'There he is,' whispered Malpractice. 'Now's your chance.'

Sir Sidney swallowed hard as he gazed at the massive muscular figure lurking by the cage. 'Does my hair look all right?' he asked anxiously.

'Yes, yes. Now go on . . .'

'I can't,' squeaked Sir Sidney, losing all his nerve. Snottless reached inside his

coat and drew his sharpest dagger. With a
wicked smile he gave Sir Sidney's bony
backside a sharp prod.

'Argh!' yelled Sir Sidney, leaping
forward on to the path. The King of Sicily
turned in surprise at this interruption and
surveyed his unexpected visitor. He looked
Sir Sidney up and down and threw his
arms wide.

'Bee-ootiful lidee!' he cried.

Sir Sidney gave a desperate squawk, picked up the hem of his gown and headed off at high speed. Halfway to the castle gates he spotted a group of people hurrying up the path towards him, and taking them to be guards he darted into the bushes with the king in hot pursuit. Malpractice tapped Snottless quietly on the shoulder and pointed to the open door of the Great Hall. The two thieves hurried over and slipped inside.

Of course, the guards that Sir Sidney had spotted were none other than Sir Rupert and his desperate crew, just entering the castle themselves. They hastily crouched down out of sight as a strangely tall lady in a green gown went crashing past, hastily followed by the King of Sicily.

'Bee-ootiful lidee, come to my arms!' cried the king passionately. 'I love-a you!'

Nanny was most indignant. 'He said he loved me this morning!' She watched Sir Sidney disappear. 'Shameless hussy,' she muttered.

'Sssh,' whispered Rosie. 'At least you won't have to distract him, Nanny. I think he's already quite distracted. Come on.'

Malpractice and Snottless had hardly located the treasure chest when they spotted a group of people hurrying into the gloom of the Great Hall. The two agents quickly darted away from the chest and hid behind some wall hangings. They watched in silence as the motley group approached, and were staggered to find that it was none other than Sir Rupert and his crew from *The Lame Duck*.

''Tis Sir Rupert,' panicked Snottless. 'They're going to get the gold, your worship.' Snottless was already drawing a pistol from his coat with the intention

of inflicting grievous bodily harm.
Malpractice gripped his arm and even in
the dark Snottless could see that the secret
agent was grinning.

'Put that away,' hissed Murk. 'I have
suddenly had a much better plan. Come
on, let's get out of here and let Sir Rupert
do all the dangerous, dirty work for us.'

'I don't understand,' muttered

Snottless, tucking his pistol away with considerable disappointment.

The two men crept away from the hall, leaving Sir Rupert's crew surrounding the chest and preparing to carry it off. Once they were safely back on the streets of the town Murk Malpractice began laughing out loud.

'Sometimes I astonish myself with my own cunning, Snottless. It is all delightfully simple. We let Sir Rupert steal the gold. They take it back to their ship and set sail for England. No sooner are they out of the harbour than they find us waiting for them with a nice little trap. We seize *The Lame Duck* and hey presto! – all of a sudden we have a new ship with the gold already on board. It is so perfect I could explode.'

Snottless took several seconds to appreciate this plan, but once he did he began laughing too, and by the time the two men reached *The Jellyfish* they were practically in hysterics.

8 Surprise, Surprise!

The castle was in a state of confusion. Puzzled guards stood and watched as a manic figure in a green gown tore past them, disappearing through one door and reappearing out of another, uttering little screams. Close behind pounded the King of Sicily, bellowing like a rogue elephant. 'Bee-ootiful lidee, don't run away! You are my 'eart's desire! Marry me pleez – I make-a you my queenie!'

'I don't want to be a queen,' cried Sir Sidney, heading for the Great Hall. 'Go away, you horrible man.'

It was unfortunate that at the very moment that Sir Rupert and his crew staggered out of the hall with the coffer full of gold coins, Sir Sidney came barging in, hotly pursued by the king. Everyone met in the doorway and for a few tense seconds everything came to a halt.

'Ooooh!' squeaked Sir Sidney and, seizing his chance to escape, he raced out of the hall, leaving the King of Sicily staring at Sir Rupert and the chest. Sir Rupert stared back and swallowed hard.

'Hallo, Your Majesty,' he smiled nervously.

The king frowned. 'Whattsa going on? Where-a you going?'

'Going? Us? Um . . .' Inside Sir Rupert's head, his brain rapidly shrank to the size of a small woodlouse and scuttled away into hiding. He turned to his daughter. 'Rosie, tell the king where we are going.'

Rosie stepped

forward. 'We're taking our gold back and going home,' she explained. Sir Rupert laughed nervously.

'Just a joke, Your Majesty!'

'No it's not,' said Rosie. 'You are an overgrown monster with hair sprouting out of your ears and it's little wonder that nobody wants to marry you. We're fed up with you, so we are taking back our gold and going home.'

The King of Sicily gave them a nasty smile. He was so huge that he almost blocked the entire doorway.

'I don't-a think so,' he growled menacingly. 'I don't-a think you goes anywhere, except maybe to my crocodiles. Guards – seize them!'

Rosie was having none of this. 'Battering ram!' she yelled. 'Forward on the double!' Muggins and the crew charged forward, carrying the heavy coffer between

them. Despite his immense size and strength,
the king was no match for the accelerating
mass of the treasure chest and he was mown
down like a tree in a tornado.

The crew of *The Lame Duck* now made
a desperate dash for their boat, while the
castle guards piled after them and the king
struggled back to his feet.

'Kill them all!' he screamed. 'Break-a
their bones an' bash their bonces!'

As the panting crew skedaddled through the king's private zoo, Rosie grabbed at her father's sleeve. 'Father, quick – unbolt the cages. Let the animals out.'

They rushed from one cage to another, sliding back bolts and throwing open the doors. With deep growls and tentative steps the lions and tigers sniffed the edges of their cages, pawed the open space and then leaped on to the path.

As the guards began tumbling out of the castle, rattling their spears and shouting fiercely to keep up their courage, they found themselves facing – not the crew of *The Lame Duck* – but six lions, three tigers, a gorilla, an elephant, a rhinoceros, several crocodiles, and a budgie. The king raged helplessly as Sir Rupert and his crew vanished into the distance.

As soon as they were safely on board, the sails were lowered, ropes were cast off and *The Lame Duck* began to move slowly and steadily away from the general uproar that was spilling out of the castle. They were already some distance from the harbour before the seething king reached his fleet of warships.

'After them!' he roared. 'I want them all barbecued, with sun-dried tomatoes an' lottsa pesto!' But the warships were not even ready for action and it was some time before the sleek men-o'-war sliced through the waves and began their chase after Sir Rupert. It was going to be a race against time.

While all this was taking place, Murk Malpractice was following his own dastardly plan of action and now *The Jellyfish* shot out from the shelter of a rocky outcrop, her gunports open and cannons poking from every side. The crew of *The Lame Duck* were so busy looking to their stern for signs of the pursuing king that they never noticed the danger lurking ahead of them until it was far too late.

'This is like taking candy from a baby,' remarked Malpractice with great satisfaction.

As for Sir Sidney, he was back in his

own clothes and although he was minus his beard he was bursting with triumphant revenge. As he watched *The Lame Duck* sailing straight into the trap he was so moved he felt a poem coming upon him. He threw back his arms and lifted his eloquent face to the sea wind.

'Sir Rupert is a pimple-head
I'll black his eye and see him dead!'

'Delicately put,' muttered Murk Malpractice. 'Now let us complete the final act of this tragedy. Fire the cannons!' With an ominous boom the cannons blasted away and cannonballs began smashing into *The Lame Duck*. 'Careful!' snapped Malpractice. 'We don't want to do any serious damage. Stand by to board.'

As the first cannonballs began whistling through the sails the crew of *The Lame Duck* started rushing about like headless chickens. They were quite unprepared for such an attack and all they could do now was panic. Sir Rupert stood on the quarterdeck and watched in dismay as grappling hooks were thrown from *The Jellyfish* and Sir Sidney's motley crew of cut-throats came swarming on board. The more Sir Rupert watched the more his dismay became a chronic illness.

'I think I've got terminal backache,' he said. Even Rosie looked downcast. The surprise attack had been devastating. It was all over in minutes.

Sir Sidney Dribble clambered on board the captured ship and swaggered across to the quarterdeck, clutching something large, floppy and black. 'Sir Rupert,' he smiled. 'We meet again.'

Sir Rupert clutched Rosie's shoulder. 'I don't believe it – Sir Sidney Dribble, but without the beard!'

'At my service,' sneered the poet, bowing low. 'We did of course meet at sea, but perhaps you did not recognize me?' Sir Sidney produced his Mad Mavis hat and plonked it on his head. Sir Rupert shut his eyes. He could not believe that he had been taken in so easily. Rosie fixed her father's arch enemy with a hard glare.

'Of course,' she said. 'I should have realized. I knew it wasn't Mad Mavis.'

'Really?' replied Sir Sidney, just a trifle disappointed.

'Yes, and it was you rushing about in the green gown, wasn't it? I wouldn't forget that nose anywhere.'

'And you got that king sniffing after you when he said he loved me,' added Nanny a trifle sulkily.

'Can you blame me for wanting the chest full of gold?' smirked Sir Sidney.

'It belongs to Queen Margaret,' Rosie said icily.

'Not any more.' Murk Malpractice hauled himself on to the quarterdeck beside Sir Sidney. '*The Lame Duck* is now under my command.'

'Your command?' questioned Sir Sidney Dribble. 'I am the sea captain around here, if you don't mind.'

The secret agent smiled. 'But I do mind. Sir Rupert, you and your crew may board *The Jellyfish*. As for you, Sir Sidney, I am sick and tired of your pathetic poetry and posturing. You can join Sir Rupert – it is your ship after all.'

'But the gold . . . after all I have done!'

'All you have done, Sir Sidney, is get up my nose,' hissed Malpractice, 'and I

don't like it when people get up my nose.
It never feels comfortable and it stops me
breathing properly. Now kindly join the
prisoners.'

'Never!' screeched the outraged poet.
Snottless drew a pistol and poked the barrel
in Sir Sidney's left ear-hole. 'Oh, well, if you
say so,' he seethed and joined the sorry
group of prisoners being transferred to *The
Jellyfish*.

With hopeless hearts and sinking stomachs Sir Rupert and Sir Sidney watched from the deck of *The Jellyfish* as Malpractice and Snottless sailed away with Queen Margaret's gold coins and Sir Rupert's ship.

Hardly had *The Lame Duck* vanished over the western horizon when a new and even greater peril appeared to the east. The King of Sicily's war fleet came rushing into view, their sails proudly puffed, flags gesticulating wildly and their keen prows slicing the waves. Sir Rupert and Sir Sidney gazed at each other miserably.

'If we're not sunk we'll be fed to the crocodiles,' groaned Sir Sidney.

'And if we're not fed to the crocodiles we'll be barbecued,' croaked Sir Rupert. For a few moments they gazed at the fast approaching fleet and then turned to each other once again.

'We're going to die!' they chorused,

'We're going to die!'

and Sir Sidney clapped both hands over his eyes. The crew began muttering and Muggins stepped dutifully forward.

''Scuse me, Cap'n, but the crew say they'd rather not die jus' yet. They don't mind a few cuts and bruises, but dyin' is a bit too final on account of not bein' able to get up again, if you see what I mean.'

'If you can't be helpful then be quiet, Muggins,' said Rosie, her face white and drawn. She had no idea what to do next, and she was very scared. She slipped her hand into Nanny's big paw and held on tightly.

9   The Final Battle

Sir Rupert expected to be blasted to bits by the king's cannons at any moment, and so did the rest of the crew, but there was not a single boom or warning puff of smoke. Sir Rupert's look of fear was slowly replaced by one of despair. He peered across the water as the warships came within hailing distance. 'What's happening? Why aren't they firing?'

Rosie was baffled too. The king could turn *The Jellyfish* to matchwood within seconds if he chose, so why didn't he?

'He's waiting until he's so close he can't miss.' Sir Sidney groaned and began praying. 'We're all going to die,' he murmured.

Nanny squeezed Rosie's hand and gazed down the menacing mouths of a dozen cannons. 'Deary, deary, deary me,' she said in a hopeless voice, stroking Rosie's hair. Rosie suddenly jerked her head away and threw herself to the deck.

'Quick, Nanny, get down out of sight!' she cried. 'You too, Father, and Muggins, before the king recognizes us. Don't you see, this is the wrong boat! The King of Sicily thinks we are on board *The Lame Duck*!' Rosie was almost laughing as her father, Nanny and Muggins all threw themselves down. She wriggled across to Sir Sidney, still standing with his hands over his eyes and trembling so violently that his knees were performing their own drum roll. Rosie tugged at his stockings.

'A shark!' screamed Sir Sidney. 'I'm being eaten from the feet up!'

'Don't be so stupid,' said Rosie angrily. 'It's me. Open your eyes. The King of Sicily doesn't know we're . . .'

''Allo-a!' hailed the king from his warship.

'Just repeat what I say and we'll be all right,' Rosie hissed.

''Allo-a *Jellyfish*. 'Ave you seen a boat come thissa way?'

'Yes,' nodded Rosie.

'Yes,' answered Sir Sidney in such a high squeak that the king looked at him sharply.

'I theenk we 'ave met before, no?'

'Tell him "No",' growled Rosie.

'Ohhh, d-d-d-definitely not, Your Majesty.'

'You remin' me of bee-ootiful lidee I

metta last night,' insisted the king.

'Tell him you're her brother,' Rosie calmly suggested.

'She's my brother,' squawked Sir Sidney. 'I mean sister. Her name's Doris.'

The King of Sicily frowned. 'You tella me you see-a boat, no? Which-a way they going?'

'No, I mean y-yes, we do see-a boat.'

'Tell him which way it went, you idiot,' snapped Rosie from deck-level.

'I can't,' Sir Sidney hissed back. 'I didn't see, I had my eyes shut.'

'To the west,' Rosie growled impatiently.

'Which way is that?' Sir Sidney was in a panic.

'Are-a you deaf, thin man with shark-nose?'

bellowed the king. 'I ask-a you which way they going?'

'Just tell him straight ahead,' Rosie groaned, banging the deck in despair.

'Straight ahead,' Sir Sidney shouted and he pointed up at the sky.

'Thank you,' grunted the king. 'You tell your seester Doris I make-a her my queen. But first, I go to barbecue!'

With that the king ordered full speed ahead and the four warships sped away from *The Jellyfish*.

Sir Rupert got to his feet. 'That was too close for comfort.' The ghost of a smile crept across his face. 'Well done, Rosie! That nasty secret agent has got the king chasing after him now.'

'Yes, Father, and if we follow the king's warships we can see what happens next.'

'But we've only just got rid of them!'

'I know, but if they are sailing after *The*

Lame Duck they won't bother us. We tag on behind, keep out of range and see what happens.'

Sir Rupert brushed deck-dirt from his jacket, and tried to look as brave as his daughter. 'All right, let's put on sail. Keep the king's fleet in sight.' He turned to Sir Sidney. 'You, sir, are a disgrace and a traitor. Muggins, take him below and lock him away.'

'You can't treat me like this! I'm a poet – a national treasure!'

'Treasure should always be kept locked away,' growled Sir Rupert. 'Take him below.' Rosie watched her father with pride.

Once Sir Sidney was out of the way, Sir Rupert and Rosie kept a close watch on the warships ahead of them. They had almost disappeared from sight when Rosie noticed several small puffs of smoke. Seconds later the faint sound of distant cannon fire drifted across the water. 'They're going into battle, Father,' she said excitedly. 'They must have found *The Lame Duck*.'

'My poor boat,' murmured Sir Rupert, who could well imagine the pounding it must be taking from the king's war fleet at that very moment.

'Never you mind, my big turnip,' Nanny soothed. 'I expect the queen will give you a hundred boats when she hears about your adventures.'

'We're not safely home yet,' Sir Rupert pointed out, 'and we don't have the gold.'

As they drew nearer they could see that *The Lame Duck* was surrounded by the king's four warships. But despite being so heavily outnumbered *The Lame Duck* was not going down without a considerable fight.

The sea was boiling with shot. Masts crashed down in every direction. A dense fog of cannon smoke mushroomed out around the thundering boats and finally obscured the entire battle.

Slowly the cannons fell silent and an eerie silence hung over the water. *The Jellyfish* edged nearer. The smoke drifted away on the breeze, revealing an incredible scene. There was not a single whole ship afloat. Instead they were all floating about in bits – large bits, middle-sized bits, small bits and tiny bits. Broken sections of mast drifted past, with sailors feebly clinging to them.

Murk Malpractice and Snottless bobbed past, lying on a slab of deck. Wet rags of sails slapped about like bits of decaying seaweed. A ship's wheel banged up alongside *The Jellyfish*, with the King of Sicily sitting in the middle of it. He gazed woefully

at everyone and then caught sight of Nanny.
At once his eyes lit up.

'Most bee-ootiful lidee!' he cried. 'I
love-a you!'

'Oh no you don't,' snapped Nanny.
'You love Sir Sidney.'

''Oo ziss Sir Sidney?' cried
the king. 'I keel 'im!'

'Oh no you don't.
You can stay down
there.' Nanny lowered
a pole and pushed the king away from the
ship, leaving him to drift off, still professing
his love.

'Look – over
there!' Rosie suddenly
cried. 'It's the treasure
chest, floating on that
bit of deck.'

Sir Rupert's joy
was unconfined. He

sang, he whistled, he jumped and he danced, but most important of all he ordered his crew to rescue the chest. Muggins was about to push away the now empty slice of deck when Sir Rupert had a neat idea of his own and told Muggins to fetch Sir Sidney from below.

'Make your choice, Sir Sidney. You may return to England with us and face certain execution, or you may climb on to that bit of flotsam and take your chance, along with the King of Sicily who is drifting about over there and would like to marry you . . . Doris.'

For once Sir Sidney was struck dumb. He climbed glumly on to the wreckage and waved a forlorn hanky as *The Jellyfish* put to sail and headed home. As she

picked up speed Sir Rupert grabbed a boat
hook, leaned out over the rails and hooked a
plank of wood from the sea. He looked at it
lovingly. It was the nameplate from *The Lame
Duck*.

10 All's Well . . .?

Queen Margaret was stuck in her couch again. She was in such a fury that she had started leaping up and down on the already broken seat, quite forgetting what had happened last time. There was a tearing sound as her stamping feet disappeared through the upholstery and she was left trapped up to the knees.

'Bah!' she yelled. Then realizing how ridiculous she looked, she hurriedly smoothed her dress and tried to compose herself. 'Sir Rupert, are you telling me that the King of Sicily doesn't want to marry me? – Me!'

'Yes, Your Majesty.' Sir Rupert squirmed. It felt as if several cannons were going off inside his stomach.

Queen Margaret furiously beckoned Lord Wetwallop to her side and he helped her step from the couch. She approached the trembling sea captain. 'Did the king say why he wouldn't marry me, Sir Rupert?'

'Yes, Your Majesty.'

'Well?'

Sir Rupert searched his brain, but the only words he could remember were, 'You tell her she ugly woman with face like-a pizza,' and he didn't think Queen Margaret would appreciate this. Luckily another memory came back to him.

'He was already in love with someone else, Your Majesty. He had promised to marry a lady with a green gown. Her name was Doris.'

'I've got a green gown,' the queen snapped back. 'Why couldn't he marry me? He only had to ask.' Sir Rupert, who thought he had found a way out of his dilemma, wondered why women always seemed so complicated.

In the corner of the room Lord Wetwallop was seething. What had gone wrong with all his plans? He eyed Sir Rupert malevolently. He had been amazed and furious when the gallant sea captain had returned the treasure chest to the queen. Where was Malpractice? Now he hissed at the adventurer.

'Yes, Sir Rupert, you could have made more effort. You knew that Her Majesty had

been pining away for love, and yet you
return without the king.'

Sir Rupert could feel a major
disturbance brewing in his stomach and the
resulting belch made a rather unpleasant
noise.

'Oh for heaven's sake!' cried
Wetwallop. 'Ma'am, do we have to put up
with this any longer? I really think we should
put Sir Rupert out of his misery by having
his head chopped off.'

Queen Margaret was gazing moodily
at the portrait of the tall, dark and
handsome king. She had liked it when
Wetwallop said she was pining away for love
and now she tried hard to pine away on the
spot, just to show that useless Sir Rupert
what a disappointment he had been.

Sir Rupert had quite forgotten the
portrait of the king and now, seeing it once
again, he brightened up. 'I don't think you

would have wanted to marry him anyway, ma'am.'

'Oh? Really? And who are you to say what I want?'

'I wouldn't dare, Your Majesty. It's just that there is something I haven't told you. The King of Sicily has played a very unkind trick on you.'

'Indeed? How so?'

'Because, ma'am, that portrait is not at all like him. Believe me, ma'am, when I tell you that he is probably the most ugly man on earth.'

'Really? What, even more so than Lord Wetwallop?'

Wetwallop scowled at Sir Rupert, who coughed diplomatically and went on. 'The king was very, very big. He had a huge mouth and his teeth were browny-black and stuck out.'

'Urgh!'

'Yes, and he had hair growing from his nose and ears.'

'I'm going to be sick,' choked the queen. Sir Rupert found this very encouraging. Usually he was the one who felt sick when the queen was around. 'I hate him. I loathe him. I never liked him. I knew he was a rat all along,' she muttered. 'I'm glad you came back without him, Sir Rupert. That was very sensible of you.'

Queen Margaret glared at the king's portrait and regally stuck out her tongue. She returned to her couch and proudly sat down, only for her bottom to disappear with a tearing crash through the hole so recently made by her feet. Her legs shot up into the air, so that they now stuck out in front of her like a strange pair of extra arms, and her dress was thrown up over her head so that she was engulfed. A muffled command came rasping out from beneath the royal pile of clothing.

'You may go.'

'Didn't she even give you a reward?' asked Rosie angrily. 'After all the trouble you went to?'

Sir Rupert shook his head. He really didn't mind. He was sick and tired of sea voyages and adventures. He didn't want money or a new boat, he just wanted some peace and quiet. He sat in the parlour and gazed at the nameplate of *The Lame Duck* hanging above the great fireplace. If he wanted adventure he could remember the ones he had already had.

'At least the queen didn't have my head chopped off, Rosie,' Sir Rupert pointed out. 'I'm glad about that.'

'Not as glad as we are, Sir Rupert,'

grunted Nanny. 'Now, why don't you sit yourself down and have some supper? I've made you something special.'

'Oh yes?'

Nanny fetched a plate through from the kitchen and put it in front of Sir Rupert. He stared at the strange mix of bits and bobs. It reminded him of something, but he couldn't think what. 'What's this?' he asked.

'That, my big cauliflower, is a pizza. Ham and tomato.'

And then Sir Rupert remembered and smiled. He began eating and a blissful look spread across his face. He was at home . . . no more scary adventures . . . peace and quiet at last!

Epilogue

Rosie sat up late that night in her little attic bedroom. She was writing a letter.

> Dear Queen,
>
> Once again you have shown just how thoughtless you can be.
>
> I think it is most unfair that my father has gone through such hardship for so little reward. He has lost his ship carrying out your orders.
>
> I don't suppose he told you half the things he did. Did you know the King of Sicily stole the gold, and my father had to sneak into the castle and steal it back again? Did he tell you how Sir Sidney Dribble—yes, Him again—ambushed us and stole the treasure for a second time? Yet my father still got it back, for you.
>
> You have been most unkind, and the least you can do is replace his ship.
>
> Lots of Love,
> Your good friend,
> Rosie
>
> P.S. You should have seen the king.. Yukk!

Several days later a messenger on horseback came hurtling along the muddy path that led to the brave sea captain's rambling farm.

'Post-ho!' yodelled the messenger as he bounced up and down in the saddle. 'Letter for Rosie Gusset!'

Rosie came charging out of the house, took the letter and rushed indoors while the messenger rushed on too, right through a small haystack, across the chicken yard and finally straight into the duck pond, where his horse suddenly stopped dead because it was thirsty, sending him straight over the beast's head and into the water.

'Oh no, not again,' he had time to yell before there was a loud splash.

Rosie ran up to her room and opened the letter.

Dear Rosie,

Thank you for your letter. Your dear father is very gallant, but a complete idiot. He never tells a story properly and leaves out all the most interesting bits. Thank goodness he has you to look after him. You must both come and have tea with me next week and tell me the whole story – properly.

Best Wishes, Maggie.

P.S. You must try my new couch. It has got reinforced upholstery.

P.P.S. I am sending your father five thousand gold coins as a reward and having a new ship built for him.

Rosie smiled with satisfaction. Maybe her father's adventures were not over just yet.

Everyone's got different taste . . .

I like stories that make me laugh

Animal stories are definitely my favourite

I'd say fantasy is the best

I like a bit of romance

It's got to be adventure for me

I really love poetry

I like a good mystery

Whatever you're into, we've got it covered . . .

www.puffin.co.uk

hotnews@puffin

Hot off the press!
You'll find all the latest exclusive Puffin news here

Where's it happening?
Check out our author tours and events programme

Best-sellers
What's hot and what's not? Find out in our charts

E-mail updates
Sign up to receive all the latest news
straight to your e-mail box

Links to the coolest sites
Get connected to all the best author web sites

Book of the Month
Check out our recommended reads

www.puffin.co.uk